THE HUNDREDTH NAME

THE HUNDREDTH NAME

by Shulamith Levey Oppenheim

Illustrated by Michael Hays

BOYDS MILLS PRESS

AN IMPRINT OF HIGHLIGHTS

Honesdale, Pennsylvania

Text copyright © 1995 by Shulamith Levey Oppenheim
Illustrations copyright © 1995 by Michael Hays
All rights reserved.

For information about permission to reproduce selections from this book,
please contact permissions@highlights.com.

Boyds Mills Press
An Imprint of Highlights
815 Church Street
Honesdale, Pennsylvania 18431
Printed in the United States of America

Publisher Cataloging-in-Pulication Data
Oppenheim Shulamith Levey.
          The hundredth name / by Shulamith Levey Oppenheim ;
illustrated by Michael Hays.—1st ed.
First Boyds Mills Press paperback edition, 1995
[32]p. : col. ill. ; cm.
Summary: Salah, a boy living in Egypt, wants to lift his camel's
sadness. So he prays that the camel will learn Allah's hundredth
name, which is unknown to man.
ISBN: 978-1-56397-183-9 (hc) • ISBN: 978-1-56397-694-0 (pb)
1. Egypt—Juvenile fiction. [1. Egypt—Fiction.] 1. Hays, Michael, ill.
II. Title.
          [E]—dc20 1995   CIP
Library of Congress Catalog Card Number 94-72255

Book designed by Karen Donovan Godt
The text of this book is set in Goudy.
The illustrations are done in acrylics on gessoed linen canvas.

20 19 18

The story "The Hundredth Name" first appeared in the
September 1982 issue of Cricket magazine (Volume 10, No. 1).

For my husband Felix, companion in this antique land
—SLO

For Peter Darrow Hays
—MH

Far back in time, in a land where kings were
once called pharaohs and the great river is still
called the Nile, a boy in a tiny village by the
banks of this river was very sad.

Salah wasn't sad because he lived in a house of
sun-dried mud brick. This was good. Mud brick is
cool in the summer and warm in winter. There
was space for everyone. For his mother and father
and five older sisters. For the three baby she-goats
and their mother. For the dark brown burro with
light brown legs and tail. For the two puppies with
pointed noses and pyramid ears.

He wasn't sad because of bad weather. The sky was always blue. The clouds—when there were clouds—were pink and violet. In his father's fields of wheat and barley, clover and maize, the sun kept the crops green and growing. River water flowed through troughs of black earth that penciled the fields. Salah had helped his father dig these ditches to irrigate the land.

This morning Salah sat by the water's edge under a low date palm, its fronds brushing the ground. He watched the feluccas with slim high sails float lazily up and down the river. Beside him was a camel. It was because of this camel that he was so very sad.

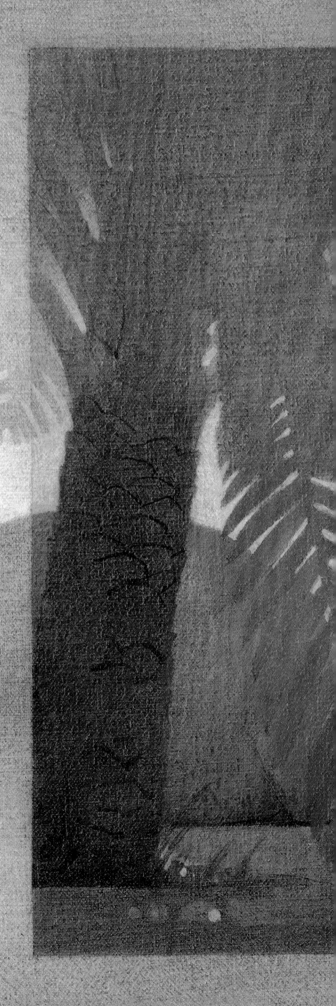

The camel's name was Qadiim, Ancient One. But Qadiim wasn't ancient at all. He was seven going on eight, born just a few weeks before Salah, in June. Salah's father had named him so "because a camel looks old when it's born, my son. Look at him. Look at the camels in the village. They all look the same. Only their size changes."

When Salah looked into Qadiim's face, he saw that his father spoke the truth. But he saw something else—sadness. "Do you hang your head because you're sad, Qadiim?" The boy rubbed his cheek against the camel's hump. "Is this why all camels hang their heads?"

The camel nuzzled Salah's leg. The boy didn't move. On a sandbank in the middle of the river, the greenshanks and wagtails darted between and around gray herons standing motionless against the reeds. It was a beautiful day, but Salah couldn't enjoy it. Qadiim wasn't happy, and of all the animals, Salah loved this camel best. They worked together. They slept together. They were like brothers.

"What's wrong with you, Salah?" His father came out from behind a stalk of maize. "You're getting to be like this camel, hanging your head, dragging along. . . ." He accompanied his words with a lightning twist on an ear of corn and a quick downward pull on the husk.

"It's all right, Qadiim." Salah patted the camel's nose. "You know how Father is. He couldn't get on without you. None of us could."

Qadiim always dropped his lids when he understood. Now his eyes were nearly closed.

Salah touched the bony growths on Qadiim's knees. They came from kneeling and rising with great loads on his back. All camels had them.

If only there were some way of making Qadiim feel happy and special. Then the camel would stand proud and tall.

It was noon. Salah's father stopped picking maize and untied his prayer rug from behind Qadiim's hump. He prayed five times a day. In a few years Salah would do the same. Camel and boy watched as the man unrolled the rug, shook it out, and laid it reverently on the ground. Then he raised a hand toward the sky.

"Prayer, Salah, has the greatest power. It is a gift we must all use, for Allah is good. He listens. He understands. . . ." And Salah's father dropped to his knees, touched his forehead to the rug, and then, stretching himself out full length, kissed its edge, stood up, and prayed.

Prayer has great power. Allah wished all his creatures to be happy. Salah's father had told him this many times. Allah would never wish a camel to be as sad as Qadiim and all the other camels. If only Allah could make Qadiim happy!

Salah's father was weaving slowly back and forth, hands folded by his waist, eyes shut.

Finally prayers were over. Salah jumped up. He would tell his father.

"I'm sad, Father, because Qadiim is sad."

"And why, silly one, is Qadiim sad?" The man smiled down at his son. This boy! Always worrying about the animals. Well, why not! To be kind is best, even if Salah did go too far with this obstinate, stupid, ugly beast of theirs.

A tiny lizard was stirring up a small dust storm by Salah's toes, searching out a way around the boy's feet.

"You'll laugh, Father, but I think he's sad just because he does look old, even though he's only seven, like me. No one in the village could get on without camels, but everyone makes fun of them. That's why they hang their heads and drag along. They all feel the same way. I know they do."

Qadiim shut his eyes and began chewing his cud noisily.

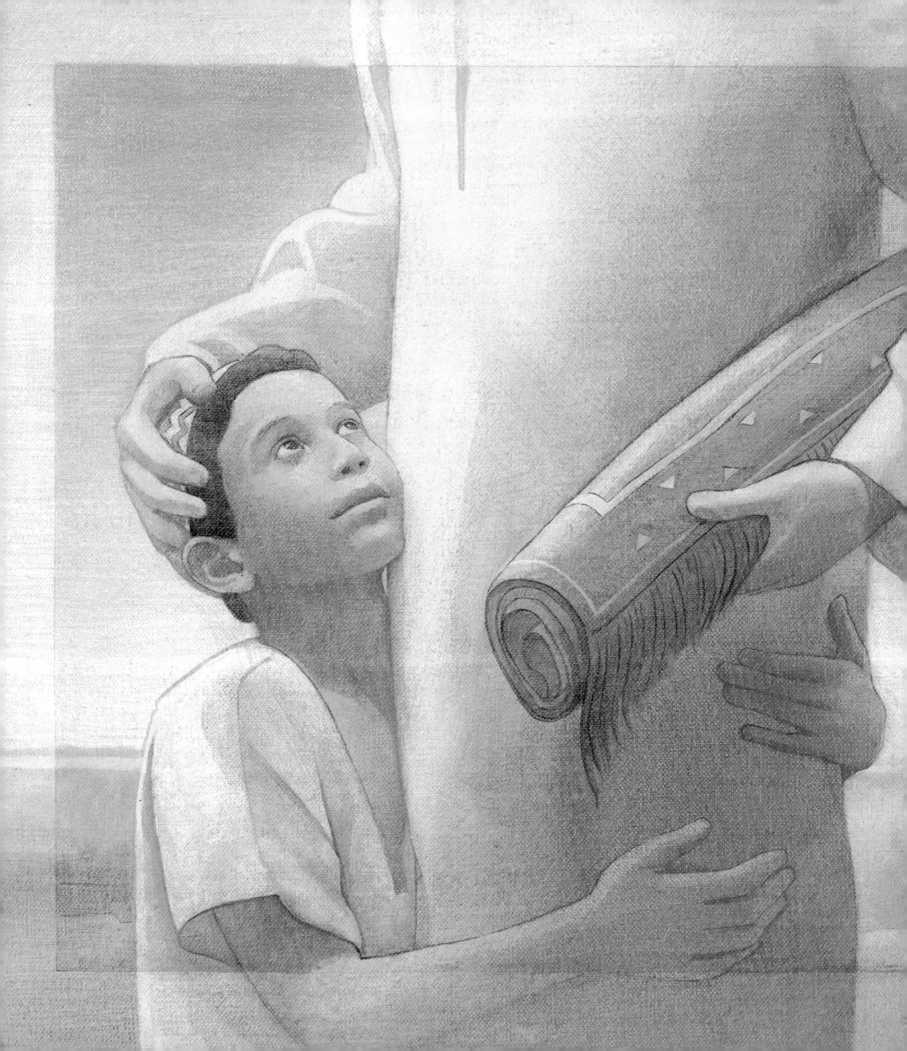

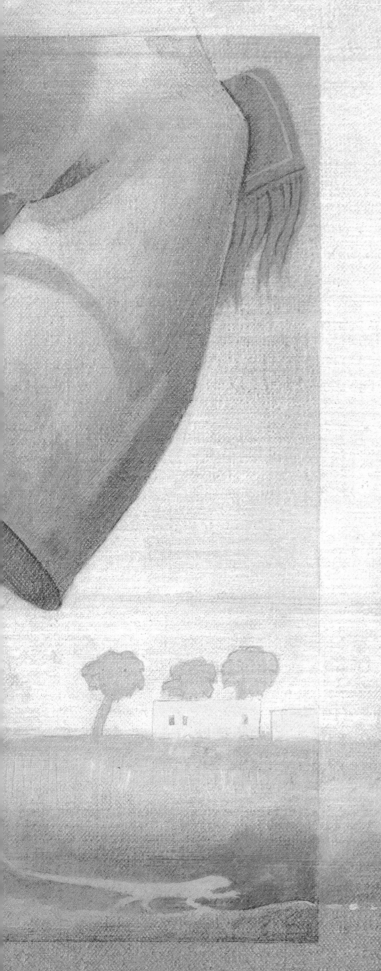

Salah put his arms around his father's legs and hugged him. "There must be something we can do so that"—he looked up at his father who at this moment seemed to soar upward like a felucca's mast—"so that Qadiim will be happy and hold up his head, tall and proud." Salah shuffled his foot in the earth, sending the lizard scuttling off. "Like you, Father. So that all camels will be happy and proud."

"I don't laugh at you, my son. Your heart is speaking. But one cannot have everything. Qadiim rests under the shade of the date palm tree, queen of trees. He eats cakes made from crushed stones of her fruit, the date. He sleeps by your side. He has your love. Think." And loosening his son's arms, he sat down cross-legged against the tree and drew Salah close.

"Here on earth we poor mortals must live and die knowing only ninety-nine names for Allah, our God, though there are, in truth, one hundred names, and the last one is the most important. And do we walk about dejected, head down, shuffling our feet? No! We work, we eat, we care for each other. We try to be happy, as Allah wishes us to be. And"—he raised his hand to the sky as he had done earlier—"we pray!" Then Salah's father got up and went back to his field.

Qadiim opened his eyes very wide, looked straight at Salah, and then shut them till his lashes disappeared. And Salah looked straight back at him.

Later that night, when the household slept and Salah lay next to Qadiim, his father's words drummed in his head, keeping sleep away.

Prayer has great power, my son. It's a gift we must all use. Allah is good, he listens, he understands. Allah wishes all his creatures to be happy. But we poor mortals must live and die without knowing Allah's hundredth, his most important, name.

What if Qadiim could be told Allah's hundredth name?

And suddenly Salah knew what he must do. Qadiim stirred. Salah slipped his gallabiya over his head.

"Sleep," the boy whispered to the camel. "I'll be back soon."

He crept to the corner of the room where his father's prayer rug lay tightly rolled against the wall.

Outside, the moon was new, like the water buffalo's horn. Salah hurried toward the river, the rug bouncing across his neck.

By the water, branches of a sycamore tree hung low, weighted down with egrets sleeping. Salah laid out the rug. Then as he had seen his father do so many times before, he prayed, his thin body moving back and forth gracefully, as if he had been performing these rites his whole life long.

He prayed to Allah with all his strength.

The next morning, after Salah had eaten flat bread and drunk a cup of warm goat's milk, he ran outside.

His father was adjusting the basket saddle in front of Qadiim's hump.

"Have a look at that camel of yours!" The man was shaking his head in wonder. "Allah only knows what came over him in the night!"

Salah saw immediately that Qadiim was standing proud and tall, his incredibly long neck curved toward the sky, his head held erect. And on his face, a look not only of happiness but—and Salah's heart gave a thump—a look of infinite wisdom.

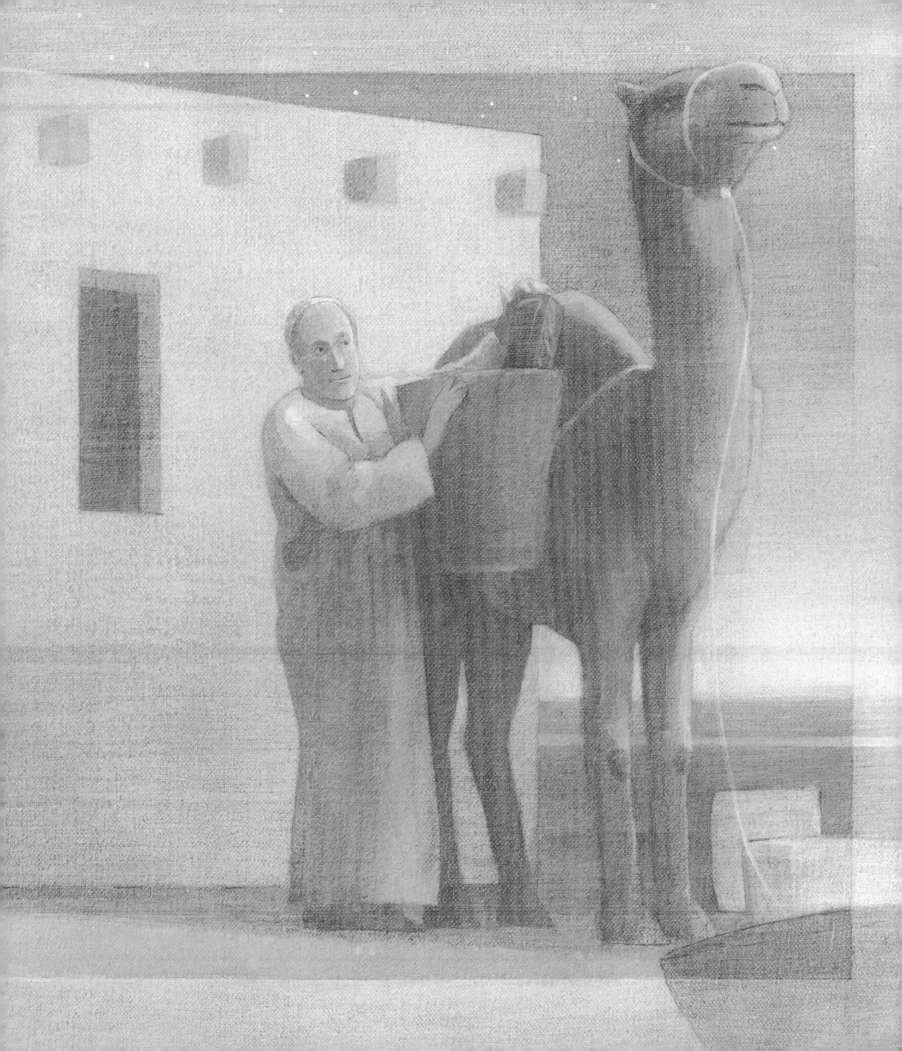

Salah whispered to Qadiim, "You know . . . the name?" And in the softest whisper, "Allah's hundredth name?"

The camel's heavy lids drooped.

"But you're not to tell. I promised Allah!"

Qadiim agreed with the slightest movement of his head.

"Only to other camels!"

Salah's father patted his son's cheek. "Go along. I've weeding to do in the walled garden. *Maas salaam.* Go in peace, both of you." He smiled. "Whatever touched Qadiim in the night, God is great. *Allahu akbar.*"

Qadiim started for the fields. His step was
quick, light, he fairly ran. And Salah, one hand
on Qadiim's neck, skipped beside him.

And this is why *I think* the camel has the look
it does. For while man knows only ninety-nine
names for Allah, the camel knows the
hundredth name, and he has never told.